Wolf Notes

Judith Beveridge # Wolf Notes

First published 2003
by the Giramondo Publishing Company
from the School of Language & Media
University of Newcastle
Newcastle, Australia

Giramondo Publishing Company
PO Box 752
Artarmon NSW 1570 Australia
heat@newcastle.edu.au

Designed by Harry Williamson
Typeset by Andrew Davies
in 10/17 pt Baskerville

Printed and bound by Southwood Press
Distributed in Australia by Tower Books

National Library of Australia
Cataloguing-in-Publication data:

Beveridge, Judith, 1956– .
Wolf notes.

ISBN 1 920882 00 6

I. Title.

A821.3

For Vera Newsom

**Previous collections
by Judith Beveridge:**

The Domesticity of Giraffes
Accidental Grace

This project has been assisted by the Commonweatlth
Government through the Australia Council, its arts
funding and advisory body.

Acknowledgements

Grateful acknowledgment is made to the editors of the following anthologies and journals in which many of these poems first appeared: *Age, Australian Book Review, Blue Dog: Australian Poetry, HEAT, Hermes, Island, Journal of Literature and Aesthetics, Meanjin, Parnassus (USA), Salt Lick Quarterly, Literary Review (USA), Sydney Morning Herald, Urthona (UK), The Nightjar: The Newcastle Poetry Prize Anthology 1998, Time's Collision With the Tongue: The Newcastle Poetry Prize Anthology 2000, New Music,* edited by John Leonard (Five Islands Press, 2001).

The poems 'Bahadour', 'The Saffron Picker', 'The Fisherman's Son' and 'The Courtesan' were published in *Peregrine*, Vagabond Press Rare Object Series 21/24 (Sydney, 2001). Special thanks to Margie Cronin and Michael Brennan.

The poems 'Exsanguination', 'Grass' and 'The Dice-Player' were published in *How To Love Bats*, Wagtail No. 6 (Picaro Press, 2001). Special thanks to Rob Riel.

I'd like to thank the Literature Board of the Australia Council for the New Work Grant which was of great assistance in the writing of this book.

With sincere thanks to Peter Boyle, Gabrielle Carey, Robert Gray, Greg McLaren, Vera Newsom and Dorothy Porter.

Wolf Note: (music, def:)
a discordant or false vibration in a string
due to a defect in structure or adjustment
of the instrument.

Contents

PEREGRINE

BETWEEN THE PALACE
AND THE BODHI TREE

SIGNATURES

Peregrine

Bahadour

The sun stamps his shadow on the wall
and he's left one wheel of his bicycle
spinning. It is dusk, there are a few minutes

before he must pedal his wares through
the streets again. But now, nothing
is more important than his kite working

its way into the wobbly winter sky.
For the time he can live at the summit
of his head without a ticket, he is following

the kite through pastures of snow where
his father calls into the mountains for him,
where his mother weeps his farewell into

the carriages of a five-day train. You can
see so many boys out on the rooftops this
time of day, surrendering diamonds to

the thin blue air, putting their arms up, neither
in answer nor apprehension, but because
the day tenders them a coupon of release.

He does not think about the failing light,
nor of how his legs must mint so many steel
suns from a bicycle's wheels each day,

nor of how his life must drop like a token
into its appropriate slot; not even
of constructing whatever angles would break

the deal that transacted away his childhood –
nor of taking some fairness back to Nepal,
but only of how he can find purchase

with whatever minutes of dusk are left
to raise a diamond, to claim some share
of hope, some acre of sky within a hard-fisted

budget; and of how happy he is, yielding,
his arms up, equivalent now only to himself,
a last spoke in the denominations of light.

The Saffron Picker

*To produce one kilogram of saffron, it
is necessary to pick 150,000 crocuses*

Soon, she'll crouch again above each crocus,
feel how the scales set by fate, by misfortune
are an awesome tonnage: a weight opposing

time. Soon, the sun will transpose its shadows
onto the faces of her children. She knows
equations: how many stigmas balance each

day with the next; how many days divvy up
the one meal; how many rounds of a lustrous
table the sun must go before enough yellow

makes a spoonful heavy. She spreads a cloth,
calls to the competing zeroes of her children's
mouths. An apronful becomes her standard –

and those purple fields of unfair equivalence.
Always that weight in her apron: the indivisible
hunger that never has the levity of flowers.

The Dice-Player

I've had my nose in the ring since I was nine.
I learned those cubes fast: how to play a blind
bargain; how to empty a die from my palm
and beguile by turns loaded with prayers –
then sleight of hand. Ten or fifteen years
and you get wrists like a tabla-player's, jaws

cut and edged by the knuckles and customs
of luck and deception. The fun's in sham,
in subterfuge, in the eyes smoking out
an opponent's call. I let my thumb stalk
each die, get to know which edge might
damage probability's well-worn curves.

See, all dice are cut on the teeth of thugs,
liars and raconteurs. I've concocted calls
those dealing in risk and perfidy, bluff or
perjury, would envy. But I've never stolen
or coveted dice fashioned from agate
or amber, slate or jasper, or from

the perfumed peach stones of distant shores.
Some think fortunes will be won with dice
made from the regurgitated pellets of owls;
or from the guano of seabirds that ride only
the loftiest thermals. I've always had faith
in the anklebones of goats, in the luxated

kneecaps of mountain-loving pugs. Look,
I've wagered all my life on the belief that
I can dupe the stars, subtend the arcs, turn
out *scrolls, louvres, pups, knacks, double
demons* – well, at least give a game rhythm.
I know there'll always be an affliction

of black spots before my eyes, that my face
has its smile stacked slightly higher on
the one side, that the odds I'm not a swindler
are never square. But, Sir, when some rough
justice gets me back again to the floor,
then watch me throw fate a weighted side.

Pedlar

Sure, I've haggled on corners with fruiterers,
barrowboys raising phlegm. I've gone on
day after day, putting forward a face I know

to be long ago cashiered of its gloss. Some
days I've buffed my face with a less penniless
tarnish, and walked out into daylight's lucrative

polish. These days who knows what's delusively
real from what's genuinely ersatz. I've carried
the faked weight of my voice through these

streets, pretending it were one of time's carats,
making claims not worth a tinker's cuss, but
smiling as if all work were illustrious. I'm sick

of the moon whose far side no gold can limn,
of the brass sales of my neighbours' shops,
of tipping dreams into bargains and watching

the stars sharpen to jewels in the ear-pins
of usurers, smoothing a look in the demoted
lustre of my pots. But I'll go on – no matter

how the world glints my loss, or the spokes
of my wheels mint out their counterfeit suns;
life declassed of its sheen. I'll just spruik up

my mock brilliance, prink up another day
in the dull patina of my pots, and call out *iron*,
scraps – as if I could believe in my own finesse.

The Bone Artisan

Just admire this ewer, this flasket,
this carafe – aren't they more elegant
than the living heads of giraffes?

A vulture's skull makes an excellent
scuttle. A hog's head a wok, or a handy
slop-bucket. This cannikin, this goblet,

this demitasse – all from a lemur's femur.
This nose pin's from a tarsier's tarsal,
this guitar pick's a jackass's vomer,

(the tiny ploughshare that divides
each nostril). No chinaware is finer
than this swallow-skull chalice, or this

crock from the head of a worn-out ox.
Don't sit on your buttock-bones like
a sharp-edged utensil – here, let me

show how this pelvis can become
a low-slung chair. Wait till you see
what I can do with a humerus; how

a simple patella makes a dish (oh,
yes say it) – for paella. This store is
full of sacral talismans, knick-knacks

I nick every day from the knackery.
I love all the bijouterie you can make
from the spine. Shall I advertise?

Backbone bric-a-brac
for altars and shrines.

The Lake

At dusk she walks to the lake. On shore
a few egrets are pinpointing themselves
in the mud. Swallows gather the insect lint

off the velvet reed-heads and fly up through
the drapery of willows. It is still hot.
Those clouds look like drawn-out lengths

of wool untwilled by clippers. The egrets
are poised now – moons just off the wane –
and she thinks, too, how their necks are

curved like fingernails held out for manicure.
She walks the track that's a draft of the lake
and gazes at where light nurses the wounded

capillaries of a scribbly gum. A heron on one leg
has the settled look of a compass, though soon,
in flight, it will have the gracility of silk

when it's wound away. She has always loved
the walks here, the egrets stepping from
the lute music of their composure, the mallards

shaking their tails into the chiffon wakes,
the herons fletching their beaks with moths
or grasshoppers, the ibis scything the rushes

or poking at their ash-soft tail feathers.
Soon the pelicans will sail in, fill and filter
the pink. Far off, she can see where tannin

has seeped from the melaleucas, a burgundy
stain slow as her days spent amongst tiles and
formica. She's glad now she's watching water

shift into the orange-tipped branches of a
she-oak, a wren flick its notes towards the wand
of another's twitching tail. There's an oriole

trilling at the sun, a coveted berry, a few
cicadas still rattling their castanets. She loves
those casuarinas, far off, combed and groomed,

trailing their branches: a troupe of orang-utans
with all that loping, russet hair; and when
the wind gets into them, there's a sound as if

seeds were being sorted, or feet shuffled amongst
the quiet gusts of maracas. Soon the lights on
the opposite shore will come on *like little*

electric fig seeds and she will walk back
listening to frogs croak in the rushes, the bush
fill with the slow cisterns of crickets, her head

with the quiet amplitude of – Keats perhaps,
or a breeze consigning ripples to the bank;
the sun, an emblazoned lifebuoy, still afloat.

Exsanguination

Ants we can always forgive; even gnats swarming allegiance;
even buzzards with their florid, yet monotonous exposés;
even snakes flooding confessions into the grass. We can
forgive him too, a boy, skipping class, believing he could
travel that day on his breath's damp visa, on the passport
of a summer afternoon. He felt safe in the marsh picking
out tadpoles among stars of the quick Conneshewan.
Perhaps, as he waited for the thunder to die down, he might
have imagined them as space modules engineered for alien
terrain; might have watched them on his pore-cratered skin,

or listened to them stutter to the night like folk violins,
toyed with them like the ganglia of an occult jewellery.
At first, only a few would have probed with their razor-edged
tubes, only a few would have hung from the underside of
his arm. He was found in the reeds hit by the hardest ball
summer had stockpiled from thunder and the Louisiana rain.
So much blood mustered out, and there was no one to tell
him not to move, to let the first cloud become the shield
to stop the others getting through. How long had he spent
waving his arms, slapping madly at himself? Those swarms

must have come at him with the noise of chainsaws, with
the ear-shattering woomping of defective P.A.s; his own
screams sharpening feedback's soaring gradient. Later,
the north wind broke through, the moon came late like
a dissolve of quinine. But who could have stood that night
on their porches, mosquitoes finding their way under the net
and screens, his blood in every smear. They farewelled
him in the burnt oil spreading across the ponds and dams,
said his name to the back-end of Spring, prayers coming
like pressurised air sprayed on the limbs of their children.

Who could have picked blossoms that night from their arms
and not have wanted to put their lips to a cup of fortified wir
in remembrance – as thunder built another column, as rain
broke from the sky, as clouds rose in the formicating weather
Coils burnt an acrid incense. Zappers publicly stuttered his
initial over and over. No one that night wanted their lintels
and sills pasted with red and black letters. They knew what
had taken him down to the marshes to tally up tadpoles, to si
by the Conneshewan and listen to looping feedback. They kno
the proper term. They know the stricken, denounced face.

Whisky Grass

Only this morning I felt anxiety's tufted leaves, and with no
scythe or sickle, I put my lips to a common roadside weed,
survivor in poorly drained soils, and blew: my tongue feeling
for the strange venation, the mid-rib ligule fringed with hairs,
until it returned the sting of whisky grass and the taste of
brown flowers. Over and over the same note matting itself
into the ground. Birds passing seeds back and forth, their
mouths, too, my tune of undoing. So many reasons to be
torn, pressed down to the seeping wound, or the salve. So
many reasons why beauty can't square up all people in this
world and give them the insouciance of flowers. All morning
my mind gone to seed in margins, waste places; held back

by understoreys of wire and the milky latex of plants no one
would give their lapsed acres for. So many reasons raising
themselves to the repeating power of our mouths. We pull
all kinds of things out of the ground; we cut off what we can
and paint it clean. We let birds pull songs through hedge-work
whose tidiness we can't attend to, let alone afford. Beauty
likes its borders green. So many reasons, deeply-lobed,
bird-dispersed, as to why the pinkest pouch in a wayside
field turns thorned and thistle-wild; why these whiskered
shoots claim my mind; and why nothing looks greener
against the rain. Sure, these leaves by nightfall might be

shredded by birds foraging among dirt dumped over yellow,
defoliated stems; the sap taken by dreams, as every rhizome
is raked from the ground. I don't know. I work a tune around
a crowning blade and let it loosen another runner, testing
the future. The wild may never give up its gestures. Not while
beauty poises itself on the edge, trying to name the place it's
native to; a tongue twisting round each bearded stalk, listenin
from the understorey for a flute-like sound, so many reasons
staking their season again. All morning anxiety's notes pour
through head-high grass. The sky turns and turns and lets
the wind in first, then rain, then light – a shiver of exhausted
leaves; perpetuals that always seem to come too soon.

Woman and Child

They listen to the myna birds dicker in the grass.
The child's blue shoes are caked with
garden dirt. When he runs, she sees the antics
of a pair of wrens. She works the garden,

a pot of rusting gardenias has given off its ales
and infused the danker germinations of her
grief. She watches her son chase pigeons,
kick at the leaves piled high. Now, a magpie

adds to his cascades of laughter as he runs with
the hose, pours a fine spray, happy to be giving
to the grass this silver courtship. She sighs,
watches the drops settle in. Today, who

can explain the sadness she feels. Surely this
day is to be treasured: the sun out, the breeze
like a cat's tongue licking a moon of milk;
her son expending himself in small, public

bursts, happy among clover where bees hover,
and unfold centrefolds of nectar. Today,
who can explain the heaviness in her head, as if
all her worries were tomes toward a larger work,

one she knows she will never finish, but to which
   she must keep adding, thought by thought.
She sweeps the petals, smells their russet imprint.
   Soon dusk will come with an envoy of smoke

and her son outlast her patience by a rose.
   Already he is tiring, pulling at the flowers.
It won't be long before they'll go in, listen
   to the jug purr comfort. He'll sleep and she'll

lie back, or get up to unhook the cry of her cat
   from the wire door. Now, a few cicadas are idling,
giving each other the gun and a cockatoo calls,
   a haughty felon. She sighs, knowing she won't

escape her mood today, the turned earth
   or its rank persuasions; her child's petulance
flaring like an orchid, or a cockatoo's unruly crest.
   Today, she knows she will need to consider

her unhappiness, of what she is a prisoner – if not
   the loss of hope's particulars. Her son soaks
the path, rinses the sky of its featureless blue.
   He is giving that water, now, to everything.

The Fisherman's Son

Perhaps it was when he first felt his shoulders
roll an oar, or when he pulled the thick boots on.
Perhaps it was when he saw the curved thin rod
of the moon angle into his father's face and hook
his mouth into an ugly grin; or when the sun
rerouted his eyes to the necks of wading birds
along the shore, as the first pink tones of dusk

uncurled along the ferns. It could have been
the way his father's knife eased out the eyes of so
many fish like spoonfuls of compote that gave
him thoughts black as the inky emulsions of squid,
a sleep no fishing boat could ease, nor star prick
with its comforting pin. Perhaps he learned nothing
from his father's face, except how whisky

trawled sleep from his eyes and left him pursued
by pain and thunder and a show of lightning's
yellow flares. Perhaps it was when he felt the rod
pull his arms through a reel's band of static;
when he heard his father's voice in the headache
scudding low across his forehead, the reel
with an insect's drumhead pitch his heart into

summer's mounting heat; the slow drip of days
revved up by outboards then dispelled by a drill
of mosquitoes, or weather finding tenor in its squalls.
Among stars and fish, those notes from the waste
hours he gutted, from the river's sweep of years,
who could know how many knives he heard
audition his nerves, or what beat his heart

took; or how many rounds of an ingoing lake
before the wind rushed into the uncaulked
cracks and left him face down, deep-drummed,
gear-slipped, deaf to his inner repertoire, blind
now to the river's weather-beaten stare.
Perhaps from a tangle of yellow air, or when
he heard the wind bale out of a speeding sky,

or a firetail add its flute to the rankling handle
of a windlass, a lyrebird weigh its call in
with an anchor's unrolling links, some twisting
erratic pull of tackle as the mosquitoes buzzed;
when he heard his father's voice in each dizzy
injected dose...All day such talk went on
as the men brought in their hauls, gutting fish

to the noise of pelicans, those bills clacking
like clapperboards, the ease of routine. Here
among the brace of tides, as wind skips along
ropes left lank and loose and dangling now
among the sloops, no one fully knowing why
a boy would desire to die...The avocets walking
the shore with their hesitant, hair-splitting steps.

Crew

Grennan steering, cuts back the engine, throws
    another squid down the length
of half the craft. Waist to neck, Davey strips off.
    His muscles build, then collapse
as he cuts the squid into loops, all that flesh
    wobbling like the jowls of aging men.

I keep my eye on a line of decaying squalls
    where clouds are towing each other
like bull-nosed tugs. I hear thunder, or what
    could be a wharf of shunting hulls.
Grennan steers again. The sea is whitecaps,
    wind, the air the sound of frigate hawks

sending out acoustic flares. These men know
    their storms: those that drag slowly
with their dredge-loads; those whose lightning
    is as quick as the fish that dart between
the teeth of sharks; whose hail's as predatory
    as the eyes of barracuda, archerfish.

This one, they say, is nothing: a gull's amplified
    squalling into an air-furnaced blowhole;
one you could shout Scotticisms into and not
    change the strength of the gusts.
Grennan hauls up more squid. Davey's arms
    and shoulders, one long tattoo,

work to a pulsing blue. Some day, like Davey
    I'll cut up squid, pull them in like Grennan.
I'll watch the night boil into a slough of ink,
    watch clouds – stacked up like hogsheads
of blackest stout – empty thick and fast. I'll
    feel my muscles ripple arrow-pierced

hearts, crossbowed skulls, mermaid-ridden
    anchors, as I pull on the ropes; crazies
all of us, testing our luck among thunderheads
    spanning skies like girders of pig-iron.
And as the rain falls, as the squid flush through
    their reds like crises of flares,

I'll call out to those men seasoned and broiled
in the stomachs of storms, legends
sung to on black-label days; men who go out in
fog thick as suet, when the sky is a roil
of hagfish and haddock, when wind is a fiend
with a suctional mouth, and when cloud

is the colour of charred *finnan haddie*. Grennan
flicks a squid's eye at me, lightning probes
the deck with prehensile speed – a tentacle's,
a trailing barbel's. Davey, half-seas over &
three sheets to the wind – throws squid ink at me,
singing verses you wouldn't believe.

Wolf Notes

I

This is the place the dogs are sent
to reconnoitre. This is the place
the dogs are sent to reconnoitre.
This is the place, this is the place
I've ached for, pulled the chain
of a long tendon and ached for.

All summer dreaming of the haste
of hounds. All summer dreaming
the leg remembers, remembers
the pain it was chained for, running
with the whelps. This is the place
where the chain broke, pulling

against pain. This is the place
of the thin, distal nail; of a moon
buried in the teeth of the pack;
of a claw broken off in the lock,
when I stretched and ached and
like prey, pulled myself down.

This is the place, this is the place
I'm a cur for, my mouth the wound
of a cruel ground. But this place
is beyond knowing. This is the place
all dogs are sent to reconnoitre,
beyond the necessities of war.

2

Go on: try to change the place
that's fathered by the metallic nail
of a single howl. Try the fence
line, the dingos foreign to it,
able to take the taste of stones.
Already stars menace the hills

with fixed arrivals, and the moon
that keeps the darkness out
with its cold arson, lights up
the folds in the dingo's ear
carrying the circumcision stones.
Men talk on faintly lit graves

when the sky slits itself open
to the drawn-out terror of sirens.
Go on: the sky has already put
down its mark, and before we'll
seek the water that will soak
the blood from the ground,

we wait behind grey stones.
In our hearts, poison and black
wulfenite in a strangled moan.
Look, all our lives we've been
baiting the wrong animal, unable
to stop because they know.

3

The moon hung like a dewclaw.
Sirius lay dogged. Even the sun
was terrierised: so far off, so beaten
back. I walked into a wind where
winter's forty-two teeth were bared
covering everything with a jackal's

breath. I felt yellow eyes signal
to a pack. In the dunged-out dark
I was mongrelised by the boned
apparition of my own face. Yes,
I was doggerelled, kennelled-out
over-whelped. So many dogmas

doggeries and the vulpine crimes
of the past. I longed for elephants,
tigers, for a leopard's or a viper's
stealth. Then, I listened deep
from the pit of the dog-watch,
from my mind's cold lair, from

foxglove, hound's tongue and from
a field of sweet, dog-eared trees –
and heard how the wolf notes
show up on the dogvane, are borne
by the strength of the dogwood,
are healed by the wolf's bane.

Dog Divinations

(an adaptation)

A dog that barks while facing the sun at the end of the day
portends danger for the ploughman, axeman, and soldier.

A dog that barks while facing south in the middle of the night,
portends injury to peasants and forecasts the death of cows.

When several mad dogs howl by night during the autumn,
then nothing evil will come of it, but if they do so at some

other time, then nothing good will occur. If a dog, after
howling in a village, then howls on a cremation ground,

then this is the end of the head honcho. A dog heralds death
when it runs away, whimpers for no reason, or else descends

into a river while it carries in its mouth fragments of bloody
bone. A dog laying hold of a piece of cow dung portends

the rustling of cows, but a dog rubbing its hindquarters
against a doorway means the occupants will become rich.

A man whose well-fed dogs fight at dawn to the east of
his house will himself fight with felons and murderous thieves.

When a scraggly dog rubs its right eye, licks its navel, climbs
up on a bed located on the roof of a house and urinates,

then a war will erupt in which all will be consumed by fire.
A she-dog who attempts sexual intercourse at a crossroad

with the King's Road, portends danger from royal enemies
in the course of that same day. A dog scratching its brow

with its right paw augurs that a young prince, whose chariot
has humbled the mighty, will be crowned with a royal tiara

and his subjects enjoy fortune and a great supply of food.
If a dog licks his penis during a marriage ceremony,

then the bride, even if she be equal to a goddess, will bring
disease and disgrace upon her family. If a dog defecates

after digging on the upper side of a house, then the mistress's
paramour is on his way. If it defecates on the lower side,

it means her husband is coming. If a dog remains constantly
curled up on a cotton pillow, then a paramour will enter

the bedchamber at nightfall. When a dog carries a mortar,
a pestle, a winnowing basket, an arrow, or a sword to a pillow,

the dog's master can be sure the paramour is in his house.
If during the dry season, a dog howls with an upturned nose,

then a stream of water will fall from the sky in eight days' time
and bring hope to all outcasts. If a dog standing on the shore

of a sacred bathing place, causes its body to tremble, then
clouds will amass, and heavy rain bring a cessation to grief.

During a game of dice, if a dog makes left-sided movements
while breathing, hiccupping, lying down, panting, or yawning,

then these dice will become prophetic. A dog that scratches
the region of its right ear with its right paw and makes sounds

of pleasure during the playing of sitars, tablas and sarods
knows that merciful kings will have dominion over the earth.

All movements of the dog's nose toward the right are known
to portend happiness; all movement and motion toward the left

misfortune – as when a dog yawns, vomits, runs away, stretches
trembles while asleep, agitates its forehead, chews on some

body part, hiccups, coughs, covers itself with ashes, digs,
wags its head, cries, hides its food, shuts its eyes, seizes on

a bone, or looks into the sun – then the omen-master should
offer incense and honey, place a hand on the dog's forehead,

and say: O blessed one, you of the deep voice, O knower
of acts, O swift one, you who are awake by night, O curled one

O lord of creatures *Om, Hum, Phat, Svāhā*, and perform
the proper rites at the solstices and at the end of each day,

and pray to all subliminal Hellhounds, that these, his blessed
omen-creatures, always be given protection in this world.

Between the Palace and the Bodhi Tree

for Dorothy Porter

Siddhattha Gotama was born in about 563BC in Lumbini, situated today in the kingdom of Nepal immediately below the Himalayan foothills. His father, Suddhodana, was king of the people known as the Shakyas and resided in Kapilavatthu, the Shakyan capital. Siddhattha's mother, Mahamaya, died a week after his birth and Siddhattha was subsequently looked after by his mother's sister Mahapajapati.

At the age of sixteen Siddhattha was married to Yasodhara. A son, Rahula, was born when Siddhattha was about twenty-nine.

At about this time, Siddhattha left his comfortable life in Kapilavatthu and became a wandering mendicant in search of truth and enlightenment. He wandered throughout the forests and towns of northern and central India for eight years before gaining enlightenment and becoming the Buddha.

'Between the Palace and the Bodhi Tree' is an imaginative depiction of the time Siddhattha spent wandering in the forests and towns before achieving enlightenment.

The Rains

The rains have washed away
the Rohini River. I look at the moon
primed and narrow as the sting

of a scorpion's tail. I know
the wind is as barbarous as a tribe
without statecraft, and I see

that mountain useless with its
crop of snow, a benign old fool
elevating itself to the clouds.

Far into the valley the Priests
are slinging the bodies
of sacrificial goats, and ropes

are hoisting above the town
the swollen eyes of garrotted foals.
Where shall I wander today

in my torn clothes? To the tip
of that mountain all I'll sense
of the outside strife; wind in
the trees, the only bucking colt.

Dawn

(after Hayden Carruth)

Beyond, towards the Licchavi hills,
smoke the colour of wolves loops
along a quiet ridge. The sky is perfect

for flutes, voices keeping clear pitch,
a koel calling through dew-fraught air.
I sit, settling into my breath, thoughts

calming, heightening distant plateaux
of dust, and the angle of the southward
opening plain. The first vulture circles,

swoops, rides another dusty current.
I hear distant tinkling, bells on greasy
slopes, women readying tea behind

faint glass. The last stars are gone,
the whitewashed moon; and from
the valley, calf-notes pure as breath

blown from sheoga wood. I smile –
smile again, because even this dusty,
yellow valley seems a basin awash

with Gangetic benediction. Not yet
am I a sorrowful man. Not yet. A koel
calls again from a silvery eastern sky.

Quarry

Today when I went to the river,
I heard the stonecutters in the quarry.

I sat a long time in the cold air.

I watched the moon gather shine
like limestone in a mason's hands.

For a long time I sat, dredging up
thoughts from the pit of myself,
turning them over as if they were
rocks capable of taking polish.

For a long time I looked into myself.

I imagined the eyes of the stonecutter's sons.

I thought of the eyes of my wife –
onyx in the dead of night;

and of the eyes of my newly shining son.

Then I let go of all thought –
and I felt like a bird
floating in the clear, excavated air

high above the talus.

Circles

I saw the vultures again today.
They descended the ribs
of an ox as if they were ghats.

I saw the moon, a desecrated bone
upon which those birds
might drip some blood.

I saw the sun slip
like ghee through a Brahmin's prayers
and death claim

its realm of circles once more
at the place
where my father weeps.

The Grove

Sometimes I listen for sounds
in the hollows of ancient trees.
The note of the darkest crow

as it rises from the company
of leaves. How often has it tried
to make a syllable out of its

heavy flapping? Only having
found the malice in its own eye
can it call out what it knows.

Now when I walk the groves
I think I hear the sweetest
sounds: men intoning vowels

into a chamber's deep echoes.
But then I hear my heart
and its target of serial blows.

O my Yasodhara! Then do
I know how emptiness makes
a grove an unquiet place.

The River

Today herons don't fly but stalk with jurisprudence;
and there's a line of retreating water where they put

their beak- and step-marks. I watch them go forward,
then reconfigure each step. Here, no cadence lifts

them through a tightening sky; but they seem to
watch the scansion lines fish make when they mouth

the surface. Today, no bird need transpose its steps
into an over-solicitous reach, or find a current through

their feet. It is enough to watch a river widen with
loose and silent evidence of a strenuous life beneath.

The Vow

I won't lie down until it walks under my skin.
I won't stop until I hear its voice,
until its tone rings through the night.

I will not give up, not until I feel its sun burn me,
until I feel its god crawl through all my follicles,

until its moon pulls itself from its diet of light
and feeds upon the circles it has given
my bereaved sight.

Brahmins – even among
the cuticles of the dead there is wisdom.
And I'll find it – no matter
who says truth can't be scratched open.

New Season

I sit in the sunshine and warm my feet.
At my ankles a small wind stirs. Yasodhara,
I can almost hear you wiping away your tears
with your sari hem. Sometimes, I dream
you've taken me in again for a simple repast,

where a circle of stars tries out the sky's
depth, where the moon pares itself down
into the smile of an obedient wife. But
then I look out – and see the poor produce
of a frozen waste, a sky soiled by its mission

amongst wanderers. Yasodhara, how long
must I bear the echoes of dhobis beating
laments into your garments, hear my heart
partitioned by too many temple bells?
I wear clothes gnawed by vermin, singed

by fire, torn by dogs, but guilt like a prison
cloak reaches down to my feet. Perhaps today,
Yasodhara, in sunshine fresh as a new leaf,
I'll simply listen to the wind tell me where
the sun is. That it blows quietly upon my feet.

The Krait

Father, remember the time I heard
a krait move in the grass? The peacock
rattled a scalding warning. You stepped
towards it, raised your arms and
declaimed a little territory with your feet.
I was scared. I didn't notice the moon,
a fang poised above my slightest act.

All I wanted was music spread out
the width of the peacock's splendour;
all I wanted was the safe canopy of
a room, not grass holding its span
of mesmerised curve. You shouted at
me to stay back, your voice pitching
its fear along a hissing arc, your feet

slipping along the breach of my
trespass. I thought the world should
be in harmony with my every act.
But when the snake broke sway
with my stare, I could see how readily
you bore the quickness of its trajectory.
I saw the grass take on ampler

magnitude; I saw the position of that
orbiting head – and as it struck – you
barred it with your sword. Father, did
I think that whatever I'd set in motion
would always be so easily set back?
Now, as I wander, I need that line
of attack, that angle of deflection –

I feel like a vector that's overshot
dimension. I long for the unrelenting
bearings of your voice, the steady track
of your scrutinising stare. Father, I
can see now how close it was. I still
remember the glint of your sword –
landing an inch from my errant feet.

One Sight

Yasodhara, if you came
to me now, I'd say I saw death

in the lattice of sunshades,
death in a sky of soft cottons,

even in the healing gauze of mist
upon the water and the rushes.

I'd say there's death too
in weather fine as your shawl,

in curtains hung by soft hands
and death in the half-wound turban

of my own smile. Yasodhara,
there's no refuge in the retinue

of leaves attending me; and none
in the swallows stitching wide.

None in the retreat of deer
to the shadows and none

in the owl's voice
low and clear as breath

blown across an earthenware sky.
None in the arbours and cool

stones. I remember your belly
round with our child. O, Yasodhara –

each night I dream all of us
are lying bloated in the lotus pool.

Monkey

(ending on a line by Ruth Stone)

All morning a gang of brown monkeys have swung
between the trees. I've had to dodge them pasting
the path with fruit and dung. They have thrown
tiny green dollops of tree frogs at the vexed visitor,

a red grivet, bending sound between the colloquial
and the absurd: its ripe screams sharp and twig-sore,
before it takes its injuries up into the forest canopy
where a python bloats among the steaming insects.

There, I see it cradle its own head: russet, fibrous,
leaking like a dropped coconut. It whimpers a long
calling toward the mountains where its relatives may
be hooting and waiting. Suddenly, I look there too

for any crude welcoming. Those distant hills lonely,
dangerous with their herds of ginger-humped camels.
And I wish, I too, had a home I could call to with
the quick of my mouth, the madness of my tongue.

Horse

Sometimes I feel like a man
with spittle on his beard, pushing
his way through dreams, mareless.

I feel the same tangle of weeds,
the same moon, a cruel spur
on the heel of the old muleless

muleteer. I go slowly where
others have lost their way, stooping
to crop water of its cloud.

There are no wide tracks, though
sometimes I believe there is
a horse who comes to nibble

my hair, my beard. Her name
froths to the sweetest taste on my lips –
before her halter's bitten through.

Buffalos

At dung-level, in the pungent field,
each one is sighing, as if drawing
up laundry like a tired old woman.

Their eyes, the blackest load,
are silted up into jellied, dirty snow.
At night they're yoked to poles

that pull me through my own
heavy slurry. Monsoonal, they bring
me strings of the grieving rain,

and bellow to the thunder, to all
the mud-born souls, to those like me
who keep falling into their river.

Tigers

What I want from the forest floor
is the smell of tigers.

So close –
that when I hear
their warm rank breath
panted into the sun,

I freeze to a shadow.

I hold my breath
then breathe without camouflage
and watch their stripes fill the darkness.

Only tigers let the light out
of the shadows. Only tigers

move into the wind
with the stealth
and odour of an enlightened prayer.

I cannot live without them.

Their furtive light
gives sense to the foliage.

Snake

They say a snake feeds on the wind,
that only a snake can see a snake's legs;
that it slides like one of the great rivers
when creeping out of its slough; that it
hears by means of its eyes; that the blind
recover their sight by inhaling vapour

rising from a snake steamed in milk.
That it can produce an antidote against
its own poison when induced to suck
venom out of a bite by a hermit,
who half-mad, prostrates himself along
the roots of an asoka tree, and pours

perfumed ghee into a hole. Vipers in
a pit writhe like eddies, and a reticulated
python surges off, as if it were the long
arc of the earth itself, slipping away
on all sides, a dark weight drawing out
the tides. How long before my own mind

becomes the votary of this slave-making
lore? It all happens so fast, the hiss
mistaken for a sudden gust, the strike
against the limbs. Then, a heaviness heading
for the heart; an old artery slipping into
a place of worship among the stones.

Dark Night

Brother, the horse and I went mad.
I felt the chilled gorges
of its nostrils flare in my mind.

When I put my ear to its hide
I heard a river drag its belly
over heretical mud. Even its eye

was loosening mine with sand.
And when I touched its landscape
of wild waters, I felt

hooves of a thundering godhead
and lightning whips of warlords
ravage further my deltas. Brother,

I cannot hold that stallion.
The moon is young yet dying. The wind
panders to a cult of whisperers.

Walk through the pyres.
Come with me to the oatgrass,
to the Ghat of the Ten Horse Sacrifice.

Tree

Above the dust, from the limb of a creaking
leafless tree, a beehive breathes.
I hear the wind move its hiss across,
and see black bees eject like flecks of rock.

A snake, its tongue a heart-beat strike,
muscles itself towards a higher branch.
A long robe of bees flows about me,
and I watch the moon hang, a septic thorn.

So many hours I've sat, and like a stylite,
kept calendar time. Now, a cobra sways,
and the bees check out along my arm.
If I stay longer, I'll have to sit through heat's

glacial noon, and like a lizard, learn to clutch
at nothing, wait for history, and look
at something more distant ... Scenes of such
little consequence, acquitted in stone.

A Vow

I vow to live with those old trees on the hill
leaning like monks with windswept backs.
I vow that the trees full of the cries of grivets
will hear only the rustle of their leaves as I sit
and pray under them until all their seeds drop.

I vow that flax, hemp, and tussocks quaking
under bullock tread will feel the kiss of the tit
as does timothy, flyaway-, feather-, and all
the swales of love-grass. I vow that caraway,
mustard, fennel and rue shall inherit the sky,

and that bindweed, burdock, beggar's ticks
and burr will know the perfume of asphodel
and the softness of lamb's tongue, while I sit
among them watching a fly make a devout
inventory of its mouthparts. I vow that as I

track into the hinterlands where folk dress
in tatters like paperbarks, and worship vines,
creepers and the shining eyes of their gods,
that the mould, the blight, and stinkhorns
on pine-needled floors will not be disturbed,

nor the pink gills of the toadstool bruised –
while I go praying to the wind, to the sticky
tips of grasses, to the wasp-quick thorns,
to the fly cleaning its wings, to bees with
legs deft as brushes, to the leaf-rollers,

gall-dwellers, to all the occult partnerships
between larva and leaf. Ah, I vow that I shall
travel as well as the dragonfly above a pool,
disappearing, as if under a magic cloak –
if suddenly a cloud takes away the sunlight.

Egret

The egret hesitates before it steps
towards an insect – it seems to wear
its stillness like a corset. Its neck
a white ceramic towards which
its mirrored knees might genuflect.
           Otherworldly, celibate –
oh, manicured object – you're some
righteous sect's uncharred lamp wick.

Overhearing an Ascetic on my way from Kosala

To find the layers you must live in the litter,
live like the flea, the louse, the botfly;
don't live by the flower, live by the fetor.

Rummage in rubbish like the crazy anteater,
no worldly comforts will ever satisfy,
to find the layers you must live in the litter.

The foul and the fetid are the true amrita.
Don't listen only for the gentle nilgai –
don't live by the flower, live by the fetor.

Don't listen at dawn to sweet bird twitter
loud in the groves from Rajgir to Madurai;
to find the layers you must live in the litter,

go with the lion, the tiger, the cheetah –
you won't learn much from an airy butterfly:
don't live by the flower, live by the fetor.

Make your home among the foul excreta;
wherever you go, follow this philosophy –
to find the layers you must live in the litter,
don't live by the flower, live by the fetor.

Brahmins

When the first cold clod is turned
at the Festival of Spring Planting
they ride roughshod over the fields
and light sacrificial pyres, and slash
the throats of sheep and oxen until
they're wild and red as the Sarasvati
when the summer garlands are afloat.

At harvests they demand rice, barley,
oats; tell us fire will carry sacrifice
up to the gods. They offer verses
by rote to the fire-god Agni; garland
their topknots with every waste
of blood. I can tell you, the smoke
with which they must appease Agni

just hurts my eyes. My anger spins
like a dust-devil on a plain when
I hear them claim they can smote
ill-luck, but only if you're of the right
clan, and can pay up. Truth should
not be the domain of a topknotted
squad who claim to have heredity's

nod to lord it over everyone. For
a price they'd demote their own fathers.
In our fields there should not be fires,
but cattle with their heads deeply
lowered. Never true priests –
just quacks from Udaya to Rajkote –
promising to take us up to the gods.

Saddhus

Some chew necrotic weeds. Some sleep
in charnel fields. Some are purified
by the putrefactive quality of time
and happily multiply in eternity's folds.
Some dig ditches and like refuse

throw themselves in. Some don't mind
the urine of town dogs. Some don't
mind their buttocks becoming sharp
as heifers' hoofs. Some are ever-walkers,
men of good sense but small gesture,

small-moment journeymen wearing
out their feet with stones. Some find
no answers in the ever-commuting sky
and lie still on bramble palliasses,
or they become ever-sitters and vow

not to straighten their limbs. Some
make leashes of their penises and walk
chastity's heavy stones. Some are lost
to an ever-administered distance,
clouds and wind their error of alliance

and so they never find peaceful homes.
Some come down from the mountains
into the searing belly of the wind,
and sit between six fires, then turn,
already blind, towards a seventh fire,

the sun. Some live sting by sting,
ache by ache, and wait for the smells
the tidal breezes bring, still not knowing
what is gathered, what is won
beyond the vermin, beyond the dung.

Doubt

Today I hear only wind smuggled in.
The moon bears down its gift-less smile.
Broken shards: a sky aching where

summer lies cut; a receptacle that might
have held – cracked, made illicit. All day
I feel fugitive, as if what goes inwards

finds sighs of a shady kind; some felony
of breath following my unsanctioned
mind. And I feel like one whose profile

sharpens in the dusk, whose hands bear
weapons because the sky turns dark.
Days are broken and detached, lost

to the wind's shifting address, and night
looms in from under a chilling breath.
My thoughts must run the interdictory

shadows, tell me to endure the summer's
face: it is what gives the world breath,
the moon its mischievous beauty; from

its charity I will receive a likeness. First,
I must breathe myself wise from embers
blown from furious, dry grass; breathe

in the wind's unlicensed truth, and sit
until the edges that implicate my doubt –
faultlessly deliver some absolutes.

At Uruvela (1)

There's never much between the tongue
and the lip of the minimal. Meanwhile
I watch worms move from here to

here across the soil. I measure survival,
make small circles. I think of the grains
of rice in my once-a-day, one ounce meal.

Some days I just want to curry favour
with the soil and live putrefactively.
Some days, I just want to inchworm on.

Sometimes, between despair and my
palate, I find what I've gleaned from
a season's slim pickings, and I bless

it with my mealy-mouthed tongue. But
mostly, I keep to myself and idle away
the time. Well, inchmeal by inchmeal.

At Uruvela (2)

(after Novica Tadic)

Yama, disfigure me. Blemish me with thorns.
Give me a cough sharp as a leper's clapper.
I will eat only dust swept up, drink only
water made muddy by a wallowing sow,
chew only reeds where the jackal has lain
giving up its life to the hook-headed worm.
Yama, twist my mouth. Make my spine
rigid and malicious as the viper rearing up.

If my legs twitch, or if I bend to find
comfort in the shade, if I lower my arms
into the warm flow of gravity, or if I close
my eyes to the sun in the middle of the day,
then tie my sins to my ankles tighter, Yama,
and place upon my heart a larger stone.

The Kite

Today I watched a boy fly his kite.
It didn't crackle in the wind – but
gave out a barely perceptible hum.

At a certain height, I'd swear I heard
it sing. He could make it climb in
any wind; could crank those angles up,

make it veer with the precision of
an insect targeting a sting; then he'd
let it roil in rapturous finesse, a tiny

bird in mid-air courtship. When
lightning cracked across the cliff –
(like quick pale flicks of yak-hair

fly-whisks) – he stayed steady. For
so long he kept his arms up, as if
he knew he'd hoist that kite enough.

I asked if it was made of special silk,
if he'd used some particular string –
and what he'd heard while holding it.

He looked at me from a distance,
then asked about my alms bowl,
my robes, and about that for which

a monk lives. It was then I saw
I could tell him nothing in the cohort
wind, that didn't sound illusory.

Four Summer Fragments

This river washes its banks
into the ordure of old repasts.

A dung beetle rolls its image
into some sweet-scented grass.

*

The moon is sky-soaked.
Red skins have been peeled.

Old Uddaka, are you still up?
Dawn is a verse we could

compose, if given twenty-one
cups of bombastic cheer.

*

Today has an easy somnolence.
Winds drift and my head nods.

This wheat is a hypnotist's chain
swaying up remembrance.

Scents mingle, then carry
me off by my disparate parts.

*

Maggots in the deer are building
temples of slime. Ants have made

their way into this fruit. And I shall
try not to think of the taste-wars

of truth, of how summer's cracked
lips can be blown by a Brahmin fly.

Grass

All morning reed-cutters swing
their arms near the river.

All morning I hear them balancing
among the perfection of those arcs.

A cold circle of sound picks up
the moon in the glint of each blade.

Each stroke comes in on the surest
wave; each blade reaches my heart

in regular rhythm. Who are these
men scything grass? All day, the moon

unknown to itself, floats like a bird;
and there's a sound too in the wind

of many imponderable things.
This river goes on. And all day,

I've listened, held between earth
and sky, wishing I too could take

my work into the cold; wishing
I too could find precision among

unweighable songs; here where
the river curves, here where the moon

dies, here where the wind eddies –
and here, where the men poise –

then scythe their absolute measures.

A Way

A winter here and a summer there
Old heron on a little lake without fish
Neither nudism nor matted hair

*

Old heron on a little lake without fish
Homes are miserable, hard to leave
A winter here and a summer there

*

Homes are miserable, hard to leave
Do not let your mind dwell on desire
Old heron on a little lake without fish

*

Do not let your mind dwell on desire
There is a way to the end of misery
Homes are miserable, hard to leave

*

There is a way to the end of misery
Neither nudism nor matted hair
Do not let your mind dwell on desire

*

A person's chest rises, then falls
A cartwheel follows the foot of an ox
There is a way to the end of misery

*

A cartwheel follows the foot of an ox
Do not let your mind dwell on desire
A person's chest rises, then falls

*

Do not let your mind dwell on desire
The aftertaste and the memory
A cartwheel follows the foot of an ox

*

The aftertaste and the memory
A winter here and a summer there
Do not let your mind dwell on desire

*

A winter here and a summer there
Homes are miserable, hard to leave
The aftertaste and the memory

Death

Something's dead in that stand of trees.

Vultures circle and swoop.
Flies fresh from the herds,
hum around my head.

I watch the maggots rise, cooking up.

Ants in tiny rows keep convoying
skin, tissue.

Even the moon can't keep itself clean:
soap soiled by a dung-collector's hands.

The carcass is a spotted deer's.

Only yesterday, perhaps,
it was grazing among the trees,

its hide so much the colour of the trunks,
it would seem to be hardly there.

How many years have I journeyed?

Time. So much its own colour.

Death in every stand of trees.

Benares

Ten miles out of Benares my feet are sore.
The forest stretched for hundreds of miles
and still I have not found my implicate law.

From the North have come rumours of war.
I see smoke rise from the Rajghat Plateau.
I'm still ten miles out and my feet are sore.

I know this road is hard and there's no detour.
Though I've wandered over so much ground
I still have not found my implicate law.

Perhaps I should return to Rajashankipur –
rickshaw it to Sakiya and the Northern Road,
but I'm ten miles out and my feet are sore.

What have I achieved that I didn't before?
What will I find in the temples and streets –
people living the truth of the implicate law

and making the crossing to the farther shore?
I know what's easy will always feel near.
Ten miles out of Benares my feet are sore –
and still I have not found my implicate law.

Eight Gathas

Hearing the jackals at night
I vow with all beings
to place my heart on the ground
as reverently as a lizard.

*

When the thorns tear my flesh
I vow with all beings
to pay what death owes
each act of benevolence.

*

On the riverbank at sunset
I vow with all beings
to chant noisily, devotedly
in honour of toads.

*

Facing the monkey's melancholy
I vow with all beings
to look squarely at the sky
and expect nothing.

*

Listening to the reed-cutter's blade
I vow with all beings
to acknowledge that my misfortunes
have no permanence.

*

When a bullock drags a cart over the ground
I vow with all beings
to remember my mother and father
and my comfortless bed.

*

Yasodhara, when your image appears,
I vow with all beings
to shatter the mirror
and bury the pieces with care.

*

Sitting under a cool moon
I vow with all beings
to find my place in the cycles
seasons enjoy with the sun.

Rice

*Suddenly I find myself asking: 'Things
do you know suffering?'* Adam Zagajewski

I can hear the farmers up all night
guarding the ripening rice crop
from the hungry animals. It must
be that some elephants have broken
into the field because the farmers
are shouting, banging copper pots,
and the elephants are madly trumpeting.
But then I realise, it is something

else: those are the cries not only
of men, not only of bewildered,
frightened elephants: those are
the cries of *dukkha*. The animals
are hungry, the men are hungry –
and they are all craving the rice.

In the Forest

So long in this forest – I hardly remember
my home. Though sometimes when I see
the pink reach of lotuses – I remember
the underside of my mother's hands.
And sometimes, when I see a scorpion

jack up the green stinger of its tail,
do I think of my father's lithe thumb,
gesturing. Sometimes the wing of an
insect, weighing no more than two
layers of lacquer, will make me count

how often I saw Yasodhara's face
under the sky's veneer. I've seen so
many lives born outside of reason; little
antennas poking through their cocoons.
Now, a praying mantis strokes the air

with a casual feeler, then tenses its legs
against the weather. How long will it sit
folded in upon itself, brave petitioner?
All day I bow to these creatures –
those who wait their cycles out more

devoutly than moons. But sometimes,
watching a butterfly emerge, I sense
my own eyelids flutter in the strange
puparium of a dream. O, I don't know
if I'll ever wake, changed, transformed,

able to lift on viridescent wings.
But as I watch, I feel my mind enter
a vast space in which everything
connects; and a grasshopper on a blade
of grass listens intently with its knees.

Ganges

I have finally reached the banks of the Ganges.
In the distance I can see the Rajghat Plateau
towards which a broad fleet of boats and ferries

take all the goods from Kosala to Benares.
They say Vishnu gave this water its limpid glow;
that this river foresees what no other foresees;

that a handful of its mud will keep away disease,
that to walk on its sands is to forget all sorrow.
But you know me, I can't agree. Yet, vis-à-vis

its beauty, as the Varuna and the Asi, distributaries
of its flow, make their way toward the sallow
plains, I know that to watch as one river marries

its waters to the other, is to see fine filigrees
of light and mist make a muslin of the rapid flow.
At times, I feel swept up, put down in a series

of anointed steps. And I know when the eddies
of this river come by in full and prayerful yellow –
I'll simply have to beg (for I have no monies) –
for bowls of ghee to pour into its tributaries.

Source

When I watch myself watching,
becoming all the more sure
as shadows weave
loosely through the trees,
knowing how they make me see
traces of myself in the sky and in the sky's multiplicities;

when the stars mount their little points along the edge,
when the moon is in its most distaff phase,
and I lose myself in a genealogy of my own conceptions,
happy,
as if the act of watching
would see me pardoned, briefly –

then, as the night moves its branch of descent
deeper into me,
and I wait a little further in the shadows
among stars that give in total magnitude to the pure keep of
this watch –

then do I know that in the distant glitter,
in the collective sigh of trees
with its patronage of little sticks –

how night keeps its pujas close;
and how in the drift of its ash, brothers,
we are not separate, nor in its smoke are we lost,

but joined, held
by any one of our God-bound effigies.

Path

The night is quiet and the fires are silent,
a wind blows away the itinerant storm.
Directionless once, but now I can orient

my mind against what's waning, absent;
I can give each feeling the subtlest form.
The night is quiet and the fires are silent,

my feet are slow, but the earth is patient,
I follow the heart like a compass-worm.
Directionless once, but now I can orient

out from my thought's divided quotient:
the depleted house, the blossoming home.
The night is quiet and the fires are silent,

and I know all earthly life is transient,
but wherever I tread I'll never do harm.
Directionless once, but now I can orient

my steps toward what's latent, salient –
though night is still, and the stars undrawn.
Directionless once, but now I can orient
a path towards an earth-less gradient.

Ficus Religiosa

Under the bodhi tree –
I vow with all beings
to sit until I become one with
all the heart-shaped leaves.

*

Under the mucalinda tree –
I vow with all beings
to sit until the moon, a bowl,
is almed only by the Good.

*

Under the goatherd's banyan –
I vow with all beings
to sit until at the root, every
snake becomes an acolyte.

*

Under the rajayatana tree –
I vow with all beings
to sit until the nests of all the birds
are given gifts by the cuckoo.

*

Under the red-blossoming asokas –
I vow with all beings
to sit until the clouds
reissue the seeds of knowledge.

*

Under the thin mulberry –
I vow with all beings
to sit until the silkworms eat
all greed-driven life cycles.

*

Under the tree hanging down to still water –
I vow with all beings
to sit until I no longer see sorrow
in moisture on the edge of a leaf.

*

Under the tree pressing me into its embrace –
I vow with all beings
to sit until I no longer want
to burgeon in paradise.

Signatures

Apprentice

It'll be dawn before the sawing's done; all night
   cutting it up, yet by dark's end, a pine,
or cypress moon, fragrant, awaiting finish. I watch

the lathed curls roll off, sinuous as beach names
   wound up in a nautilus. I love the axe's
deskwork prose, the four grades of night sky,

the thunder brought into sync with the cross-grain
   gnarls. All night I work under lightning's
rough-edged saw. I rub at the rings, polish each

stump to a peak of well-logged summers. All night
   getting a rhythm, sealing time under resin,
my sweat mixing with the dust, the saw singing

as it hits a burl, sandpaper lending wood a choice
   of stars. Though I'm sore from the sticking
blades, though my heart is like a buck, rubbing

antlers on bark, though my hands seek concert
   with the dark, by morning's first spill,
no stroke will be unrung, no tool-teased curl will

lie unswept, or be taken by wind; no wing-sown
　　whorl loom up to the levelling sun.
I love the silent gnarling, the ingrained refusals;

designs hewn from skies hardened by a splintering
　　glaze; sighs knurled into curses, moon-edged
rehearsals; words curling off a lumberman's tongue.

All night listening to the wood crack, to the saw
　　keen back. My heart coming hard again –
& again if the shrill stars of summer have sung.

An Artist Speaks to his Model

What can I ask of your lips
that they haven't already given
my colourless signature; of your
hands other than to shade
your eyes as the sun burnishes
the windows, then carries on
to the grey porticos of the square.
I see pigeons on the gold-lit roof
of the Cathedral of St Christopher,
and as I stir my brush about
my palette – scarlet is what
I pray for; scarlet that flows under
a vanquished bridge; that lives
with finches in the tops of trees
because, desire, you said,
should always live on the wing.
As I hold my brush, your skin
is a breaking wound. I could
mend it with all the things
I know I'll one day lose, but
now I imagine you're only one
red facade away from my slender
stairwell, lindens and chestnuts
dropping their blossoms onto
the street. Elise, I know you live

by endless esplanades, by fierce
pigments, by the rich gilt with
which you shine your dreams
into the colour of absent things,
but we belong to rooms, Elise,
whose heat prompts curtains
to blow, and the skin to seek
communion with the blue-black
night. Sometimes I don't know
what is memory, what dream.
Last night through the slant beat
of the rain, I thought I saw you
leaning against an easeled arch,
a vertigo of colour sweeping
your face. Elise, my heart is
placed before the marble steps
I would have you reach, but
I know nothing can capture you.
Perhaps only the muted leaf
the wind takes. I search all
the shades the wind might bruise
you with, days in these bitten-out
streets. Impossible to get your
lips to resemble fate. Soon,
the pine limbs will disorder

my yard, the load of needles
shake loose, and the finches
peck at seed dropped by women
whose hands – dark, serene –
tend an earth whose lilacs are close.
Elise, around your shoulders
I'll paint blood. Around your
breasts an emergency of leaves.
I'm waiting for the light to be
cornered on the sill. I'm waiting
for your voice to short out my
heart along the quickly burning
length of St Christopher's spire.
Already an unthankful moon
has climbed opposite the sun.

Sailor

I've seen the heavy beauty of a storm's
boil of black over the east. I've felt the moon
peeled and pulling. I've stared into the night,
and woken each day with the sun,
same old dog at my feet. I've loved
the guttings, the lies, the slicks, cold turning
each breath into its ghost. I've gone each
day into unfledged light,
a red-tailed tropic bird preening a plume,
a gull hitching a winched cry over a merciless
latitude. I've known the shearing edge
of the wind, and the horizon,
that scurvied gum-line, turning scornful
as a seafarer's grin. I've heard a rowlock's
cadence-clipped suck of my breath down
a fathomless hole; and listened
as storms weighed in: a wharf of shunting
hulls. I've seen the sky roil as if a pod
of loggerhead turtles swam against the chop
and filled their mouths
with tentacles. Without recompense
or ballast, I've followed the peregrine moon.
Though lines slacken, fall back, keels lisp
a slick wake, days become
sea-shapes pincered to the bait, I've gone

each night into the salt-whitened ache, into
older stings of time and hope. I've looked
into the grace that endures in
blue air, that slips again and again between
my fingers. I can tell you, that in the harbour
the yachts sway and drift in and out
of narrow channels, that the rope
I hold is only as tremulous and purposeful
as the words sailing nowhere. I hold to them –
as the rain hits with heavy-sinkered lines,
as the birds rearrange
their feathers, as the light that was
beautiful once, becomes just another deepening
shadow; and, as my hands pay it in:
each inch of an unbailed sky.

The Courtesan

1

Dark was just coming on. Lightning flexed
its muscled whip. The rain fell in heavy drops.
Steadily, the clouds puffed up. Many times

I thought I knew the predicted outcome.
I thought I knew the way the evening would
turn out, sure and tight – a monkey's tail-ring.

2

These ascetics with their vainglorious celibacy.
They come to my door with their alms bowls.
At first they have downcast eyes. I like to

play a game: I fill their bowls not with food –
but with water's mirror. When they see
my face reflected, then they thirst. And,

as I turn to go, they beckon me, sated by
so much sun, begging me to stay, before
some icy penitence reseeds their ground.

3

Today, the fishmonger comes with his vanilla
scented breath. How shall I bear him, slippery
as water? I laugh at him and his vinegar eels.

And later, the gaze of that poppy-seed seller
will work itself into my clothes. At least
he's better than the thistle-lopper, whose eyes

latch onto my skin like beggar's ticks, or lice
sewn down without tenderness. Afterwards,
I prickle and smart, then feel numb for hours.

4

Who he was I couldn't say. Not the usual man
who wants to be worked with casually: his
routine hardness placed in your working hand.

O, how I'll remember him under the weight
of the mill-stone maker, the grain-sack puller,
the mausoleum attendant with his callous breath.

Even under the pulverising weight of the mortar
and pestle maker, who comes to me cold and
anxious – hoping I'll make easier work of his son.

5

I once thought this life to be good as any other.
I'd look up at the sky and assess the weather:
at least there'd be those rain squalls of luxury.

Now, only empty-handed sky, and tufts
of thin, disappearing cloud...O, how I still look
for thunderbolts in the silk-unraveller's hands.

6

No matter how hard I clung I felt the tip
of lightning extinguish my hold. I felt the wind
push. For the first time I felt my body slip,

I felt thunder scud...Then, suddenly I felt
cold, utterly mizzled on. I felt the doldrums
blacken the eye of the storm...Then,

I began staring out into long snowdrifts –
as if I'd become a woman who can command
a season to leave when she narrows her fan.

7

Here, moodily watching my scarlet carp.
Sometimes, a band of sunlight strikes and I can
see into their dark insides. They flit quickly

about the knife-edge light, as the eyes of these
men do, trying to pare away my smile, the one
I paint on with red. But they know the shape

my tongue has in the thick green depths.
And I know the taste of them, pressed into
me bitter as weed, over which these waters pass.

8

He loved best my aviary. He'd spend hours
teaching those parrots songs and palindromes.
One day when a pangolin got into the bantams

he composed a most beautiful dirge. Strangest
man, happiest amongst birds. All he wanted
of me was to recline each evening on a bed

of owl and linnet feathers. Later, he developed
a passion for oriental fowl. I began to feel
outclassed by the guinea hens. So I dismissed

him, regretting it a little...I still miss the way
he'd speak to those parrots, teaching them his
sonnets and how to repeat them backwards.

9

Poetry, never one of my accomplishments,
came to me one day in the yard. I can no better
explain it than I can the wind blowing its bell-like

scales into these chimes. I can't remember what
I composed, only that my voice seemed to turn
into a wind-crafted charm...I think of it on dull

afternoons, abstractedly reciting from a canon
of ghazals to some pewter maker's ignorant sons.
I hope for a glint, some further crystalline tune

to turn my tongue away from this routine tang,
from these faces, which, on hearing anything near
to poetry, turn the separate greys of lead and tin.

10

When I'm feeling desolate, I recite the names
of winds: *haboob, sirocco, zonda, simoon.*
Sometimes, when unkind hands take me in

to their whirlwinds, I say: *saistan, dust storm,
mistral, typhoon.* I don't know why, but in
these atmospheres of power and guilt, I try

to look into the eye-wall of the hurricane and
shout out to the forces of deflection. I'm sick
of my words evaporating into pale skies and

into the false dawns of blandishment. I'll wait
for the monsoon-predictor, his head always
true, and homing in like a pilot balloon.

The Superintendent of Pastimes

Paint your body with fragrant paste. Fumigate yourself with incense smoke and close the windows of your house. It is the Season of Early Dew, and you must wait before you can sit on the terrace and receive the warmth of the rising sun. Soon, soft breezes will begin to blow and a fleet of high, broad ships arrive, and you will receive gifts of palanquins, sleeping cots with jewelled legs, golden betel boxes, camphor and silks.

In the Rainy Season, when the clouds ramble and the trees spread their fragrances, and the ground is covered with soft mosses – the yellow, black and red liqueurs will be served. It is then that I shall blow a tune into my conch shell and request the cuckoos to sing, the black bees to hum. It is at this time too, that I shall ask you to inspect yourself for the marks of your lover's teeth; that you orate the comforts as described in the Seventh Canto, that you paint your breasts; that you recite from the Breviary of Bawds and Rakes; that you cut out designs on lotus leaves and place them in a boat to reach the Ganges; that you dance, indifferent to worldly things; that you become assiduous in the use of go-betweens in passages of coquetry; that you become vigilant of buffoons, hangers-on, misfeasors and cheats.

In the Month of the Two Full Moons, if you spend it with a fellow from nowhere, a wastrel whose face is his fortune, you will offend several admirers and most likely pauperise yourself. It is here, at this juncture in the year, that I may need to sermonise on death-defying truculence, on flattery of the strong, and blandishments to the weak. Then, out of weeping mud, with my docked and whittled breath blowing once more into the conch – I shall ask, before the month ends, that you give your evenings to reflecting upon the interrelated chances of misery and money.

During the Festival of the Brain Fever Bird, anything sinfully stolen has to be returned to its owner, anything honestly earned must be given to the gods. Look, already it is the Season of Fallen Stars – and there is a river asking what is this through which I flow?

Soon, the Modest Season of Phantasmagoria will arrive, and yes, I shall bring to you the nightingale that has fallen from its tree. And at last, when the Supernal Equator is eclipsed by the sun, you will fit jasmine chaplets to your hair and wear earrings of Palmyra frond and laugh in uproar as you walk the streets. Then I will hand you baskets of leaves, and you'll bathe in the tanks that I have ordained within the gardens of your home, before it is the Month of Winds with Fragile Chimes in the Season of Ephemeral Snows.

At Dusk

The lightning gets busy this side
of silence, and when the moon
    appears from among a few wind-nicked
        clouds, she will hear the crows
        as they fly westwards like the dark
debris of the fruit bats testing every threshold.
The earth is not yet a bell ringing
        for the lost, only what's left
    under the boards of the porch that take
the heavily repeated riffs of a guitar, Janis
Joplin haemorrhaging through a hi-fi.
        Smoke from her cigarette
    is coiling close to the faint sheen of her lips.
Static sizzles, and there's the sound of a zapper
    short-circuiting the lives of moths
        and midges, though she thinks
    only of the soundless storms of love
her lips are giving lyrics to. Noise, quiet as
    it is kept, is not what she wants of the dusk,
        but she turns up the sound,
    and plays to the thunder. She rocks
and hums, and her voice is the shadowy
    foliage where spiders live, suspended
        in time. She thinks how she
        yields each night to the assassin bug's

blue spit; everything saying she needs Joplin's
flyblown whine, cicadas holding
the pedal down. Inside,
there's nothing but husks, dry leaves
blowing towards the back of her life, drumfire
igniting like a headache. Two fence posts
away, a cat defines with its wail
one point of speech. Insects are still
building their head of steam. She can hear
traffic's burr, feel the tap of her pulse
like a trapped ghost,
feel longing string height to her blood,
an implacable gnat, a bug that never
lets up. Soon the muddy voices will
ooze back, guitars that licked
the air with hottest lightning, wait once
more. Then she'll hear the crickets start up
in the earth, and she'll sit with herself
in the dark, listening to the rain
fall across the path, to mosquitoes etch
long cries, before a stylus winds its way
inwards again, and she hangs in its
tight web, safe with what she hears.

Notes

The Lake: the italicised phrase 'like little electric fig seeds' is from a poem by Charles Wright from his book *Chicamauga* (Noonday, 1995).

Dog Divinations: contains lines culled from the *Sarngadhara Paddhati* which I have edited, rewritten and reassembled. *Sarngadhara Paddhati* (Sarngadhara's Guidebook), is a medieval encyclopaedic anthology written by Brahmin priests. The relevant section is chapter 83, the 'science of omens' from which Verses 1–120 have been reproduced in 'Predicting the Future with Dogs', by David Gordon White, in *Religions of India in Practice*, ed. Donald S. Lopez, Jr. (Princeton University Press, 1995).

Wolf Notes 2: partially inspired by Pimone Triplett's poem, 'Self-Portrait as a Dream of Giving up the Child' – section 3, from *Ruining the Picture* (Triquarterly Books, 1998). I have adapted some images in the opening lines.

Dawn: the last stanza owes a debt to Hayden Carruth's poem 'Twilight Comes' published in *The Antaeus Anthology*, ed. Daniel Halpern (Bantam Books, 1986). I have adapted some images.

Monkey: 'the quick of my mouth,/ the madness of my tongue' is from Ruth Stone's poem 'Poems' published in *In the Next Gallery* (Copper Canyon Press, 2002).

Tree: owes a debt to William Stafford's poem 'At the Bomb Testing Site' published in *Contemporary American Poetry*, ed. A. Poulin, Jr, 3rd edn (Houghton Mifflin, 1980).

At Uruvela (2): inspired by Novica Tadic's poem 'Antipsalm' published in *The Vintage Book of Contemporary World Poetry*, ed. J.D. McClatchy (Vintage Books, 1996). Yama: god of death.

Rice: a partial adaptation of a passage in Michael Carrither's book *The Forest Monks of Sri Lanka* (Oxford University Press, 1983).